For my children, Nicky and KJ,
who never pay attention.
M.J.

For Miguel.
K.L.

Scholastic Children's Books,
Commonwealth House, 1-19 New Oxford Street,
London WC1A 1NU, UK
a division of Scholastic Ltd

London • New York • Toronto • Sydney • Auckland
Mexico City • New Delhi • Hong Kong

First published by Scholastic Ltd, 2000

ISBN 0 439 01168 X

Typeset in Horley Old Style

Printed in China

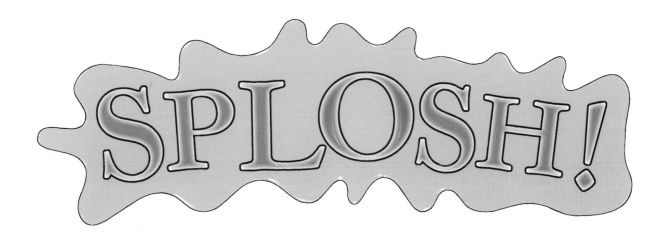

by

Mike Jubb

illustrated by

Karin Littlewood

SCHOLASTIC
PRESS

Our Dad should have been a clown. He's always clowning around. Especially when we're out with him, we can never be quite sure what's going to happen next.

He walks along walls, balancing like a kid.

He dances with his own reflection in the shop windows.

He climbs up lamp-posts and shouts, "I'm the King of the Castle!"

Once, he even kissed
a cardboard cut-out
of a beautiful lady.

Sometimes, we try to pretend
that he's not with us when
we're out with our Dad.

Last week, we were walking home from the
shops with our Dad. It had just stopped raining.
"Sam, please don't walk
through the puddles,"
Dad said to me.

"I *wasn't* walking through
the puddles," I said.
"Yeah, he *wasn't* walking
through the puddles,"
said Claire.

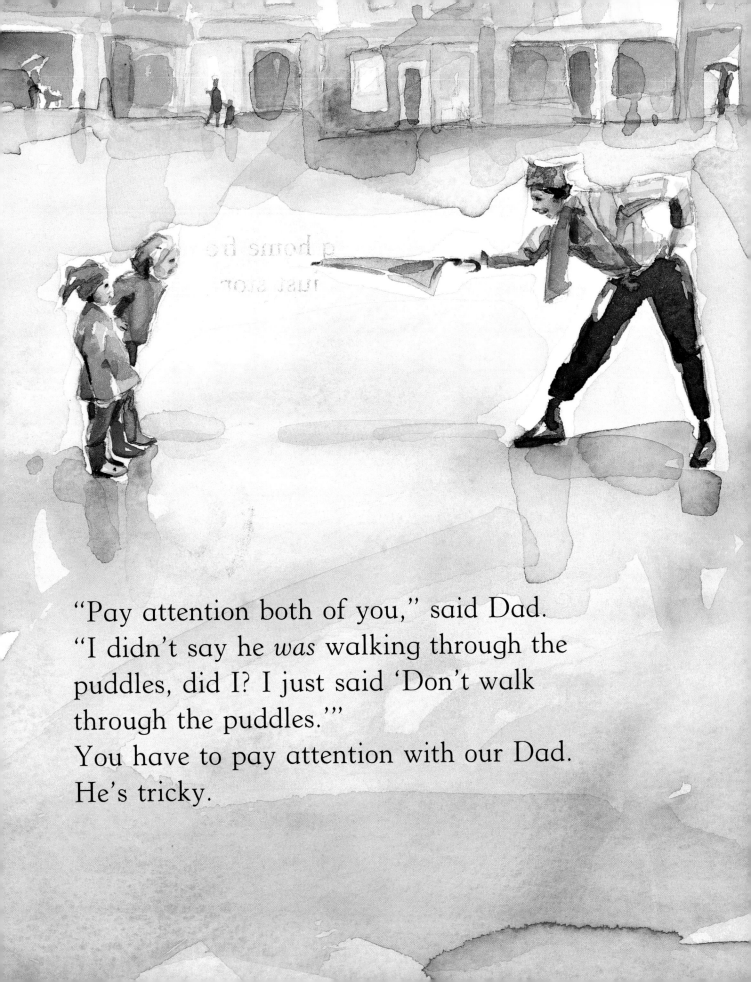

"Pay attention both of you," said Dad.
"I didn't say he *was* walking through the puddles, did I? I just said 'Don't walk through the puddles.'"
You have to pay attention with our Dad.
He's tricky.

Then Dad walked right
through the middle of a puddle.
"Dad, *you're* walking through
the puddles," said Claire.
"Yeah, *you're* walking through
the puddles," I said.
Dad stopped and looked at me.

"Who said it had to be fair?" said Dad laughing, as he walked through another puddle. "And anyway," he said, "you're still not paying attention." He stopped and looked at Claire. "I didn't tell *both* of you not to walk through the puddles," he said. "I just told *Sam* not to walk through the puddles."

Claire licked the sugar from
around her lips and grinned.
"Oh, I get it," she said. "Does
that mean that *I* can walk
through the puddles then?"
"Yes, of course you can," said Dad.
So she did.

"Hey, that's not fair," I said.
"Sorry, Sam," said Claire, "but who said
it had to be fair?" And she walked through
another puddle.
I started to sulk.

"Don't splosh," Dad said to Claire.
"I *wasn't* sploshing," she said.

"Pay attention," said Dad. "I didn't say you *were* sploshing, did I? I just said 'Don't splosh.'"
He went into the shop to buy a paper.

Well, this time, I *was* paying attention.
Dad didn't tell *me* not to splosh, so when
he came out again, I sploshed him hard.
"You didn't tell *me* not to splosh," I said.
Dad grinned. "*Now* you're getting the idea,
Sam," he said. And he sploshed me back.

"But that's not fair," said Claire. "If *Sam*
can splosh, why can't I? *I* want to splosh."
Now *she* was starting to sulk.
"Sorry, Claire," I said, "but who said it had
to be fair?" And I sploshed her. So did Dad.

Claire doesn't sulk for long. She fights back.
"Well, I don't care *what* you say," said Claire.
"If you two are going to splosh *me*, then I'm
going to splosh *you*." So she sploshed me back.
And then she sploshed Dad.

"Right, that does it," said Dad. "This calls
for some BIG sploshing."

Just then, a van drove past splashing through a huge puddle in the road. Dad got soaked!

"Well, you said you wanted some
BIG sploshing," said Claire.
"But you weren't paying attention,
were you?" I said to Dad.

Our Dad should have been a clown.
He's always clowning around. We can never
be quite sure what's going to happen next!